PETER PUCK

and the

STOLEN STANLEY CUP

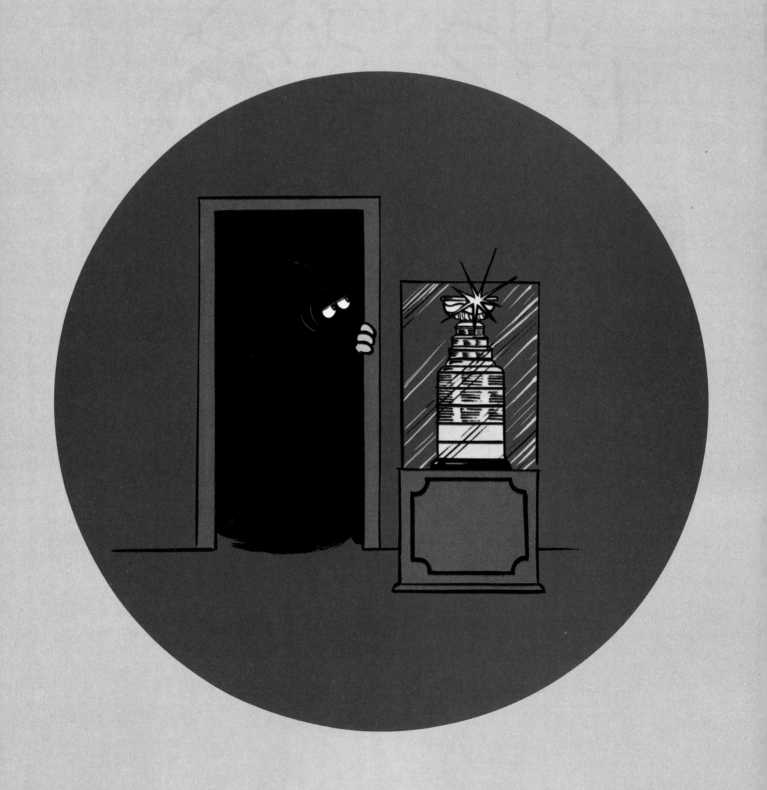

PETER PUCK

and the

STOLEN STANLEY CUP

by Brian McFarlane

Drawings by Bill Reid

THE
LIBRARY
SHOPPE

Canadian Cataloguing in Publication Data

McFarlane, Brian, 1931-
    Peter Puck and the stolen Stanley Cup

Issued also in French under title: Peter Puck et le
vol de la coupe Stanley.
ISBN 0-919161-00-6

1. Hockey - Juvenile fiction. I. Reid, Bill, 1930-
II. Title.
PS8575.F37P47   jC813'.54   C80-094545-X
PZ7.M32Pe

Printed in Canada by RBW Inc.

Contents

Introduction

My fast little friend, Peter Puck, has turned detective. Hockey's most prized trophy, the Stanley Cup, is gone. Who could have taken it? How did the thief get away? Will the cup be recovered in time for the final game?

The hockey world is upset and alarmed. Fans, players and league officials count on Peter to solve the mystery. Over the years, the imp of the ice has played a key role in hockey's most amazing events but he's never had to deal with a robbery.

Will Peter solve the crime? Wish him luck. Cheer him on. The little puck detective needs all the support he can get as he begins the biggest adventure in his life.

Brian McFarlane

1 The Scouts and the Warriors

"Brrr . . . it's cold in here," said Peter Puck, shifting his round rubber body to a more comfortable position on the freezer shelf.

"I know hockey pucks have to be frozen before every game," he grumbled. "It makes us slide faster on the ice. And it does take some of the bounce out of us. But that doesn't mean I have to like it."

No, Peter Puck didn't enjoy sitting in the cold at all. Most of the time, he'd simply grin and bear it, accepting the sub-zero temperature the way any hockey puck would. It was just one of those things he had to do to be a big league hockey star.

He tried not to think about the thin layer of frost that covered his tough rubber hide and dreamed about the game just minutes away. Any second now the referee would come to get him. Then he'd be a star again in a Stanley Cup playoff game. He'd be back on the ice where he belonged, with strong men from two great teams chasing him around the arena, passing him, blocking him, zapping him into the net. Oh, it's fun to be a hockey star . . . everyone knows who you are!

It was the sixth game of the Stanley Cup playoffs between the Scouts and the Warriors. Like everyone else who was a part of the action, like the players and coaches . . . and even the fans . . . Peter had a case of pre-game "jitters." He was shivering anyway because of the cold air in the freezer, but deep inside his rubber body he could feel what the players called "butterflies." It was a funny fluttery feeling that felt like . . . well . . . like butterflies. Just about everyone at the arena that night had the butterflies — even the bouncy little puck.

Just then, Peter heard footsteps outside his chilly icebox. There was a knock on the door, and a voice called through to him:

"Tell me, great hockey star, am I in luck,
Is this the frosty home of Peter Puck?"

Peter chuckled. It was the voice of his favorite referee, George Phair. So Peter called back:

"Open the door and see for yourself,
Then help me down from this icy shelf."

The door was opened and George Phair grinned in at Peter.

"Hi, Pete! My, you do look cold. Let me get you out of there. It's almost

4

faceoff time, so we'd better hurry. There are about 18,000 fans out there waiting for me to get the game underway."

"I'm ready," replied Peter. "And if the Warriors win tonight, it'll be the end of another long hockey season. Do you think they'll win, George?"

"I gave up trying to figure out who was going to win a long time ago," said the referee as he carried Peter down the long corridor that brought them to the rink. "I'll say this, though. Those Warriors are tough. They need one more win to capture the Stanley Cup, and the chances are good that they'll do it tonight."

"I know you don't let yourself have a favorite team," replied Peter. "And neither do I. Still, it seems to me that the Scouts are better sports. And they have some fine young players. That fast centerman, Steve Swift, can do wonders with me when he gets me on his stick."

"Yes, Swift's a good one," said the referee. "But he'll have to live up to his name tonight and score a few goals if the Scouts hope to force a seventh game.

Don't forget that the Warriors are playing on home ice. And they have those bruisers, Slugger Simpson and Crash Cranston, on defense. They're going to be hard to beat."

"And then there's Butch Burns, the goalie," added Peter. "Maybe I shouldn't say this, but he really is mean. The other night, when I just trickled into his net, he whacked me with his big old goal stick and zapped me down the ice. I hope he's in a better mood tonight."

"You'll know soon enough," was George Phair's answer. "But don't count on it. Burns is a tough one. Well, here we go, Peter. It's game time!"

The referee skated out to center ice, holding Peter high over his head, and blew his whistle.

The bright lights were almost blinding. The crowd roared. Peter was so excited that he forgot all about the jitters. Then the teams skated into position, George Phair's hand moved over the sticks of the two players facing each other at center ice, and Peter was sent flying to the ice surface. He flashed in between the stick blades and the battle was on.

Whack! Zap! Crunch! The players attacked him with all their might, but Peter didn't mind. He was right where he belonged, in the middle of an important hockey match, where each team was trying its best to win the game. He relaxed and enjoyed every second of play as he whirled around the ice. Sticks poked at him, players flew through the air in front of him. He caromed off skates, pads, and the boards. Early in the game, he was sent flying towards the goal, and bounced off the goal post with a "thwaaang" that could be heard high up in the arena. Moments later, he hit the protective glass behind the goal with such speed that several fans screamed and ducked away,

afraid that Peter might crash through the glass and injure some unlucky spectator. But the glass didn't break. Peter tumbled back to the ice and the game went on.

Peter and George Phair, the referee, were right about the Warriors. They were a nasty group of hockey players. And tonight, playing in front of their noisy home town fans, they were even nastier than usual.

They chopped and tripped and held, and even though George Phair always handed out penalties when the Warriors broke the rules, they seemed to be in control of the game.

Whenever the Scouts came near the Warriors' blue line, they were greeted by big Slugger Simpson and Crash Cranston. It was the sort of meeting one only sees on a hockey rink . . . or in a riot.

Crash and Slugger piled into the lighter Scout forwards. They crunched the Scouts to the ice, using shoulder, hip, and anything else that would bring a Scout player down, especially if the referee happened to be looking the other way.

Butch Burns, the Warrior goalie, enjoyed the rough play.

"Sic 'em, Slugger! Give it to 'em, Crash!" screamed the goalie. "Zap 'em like that and I'll have my shutout and we'll win the Stanley Cup. Ho, ho, ho. That's the way to go!"

Every so often, when a faceoff was in his zone, Burns would slide his face mask high on his head, stretching the bright red straps that held it in place, and make fun of his opponents.

"You guys will never beat me. Just try sending Peter Puck my way and I'll knock him bowlegged!" He stuck out his tongue at Peter.

The Scouts *did* try shooting Peter at the Warriors' goal. But for two periods they had no luck at all. And the harder they tried, the harder Butch Burns laughed at them.

"Oh, you hot shots!" he screamed. "Can't even get a good shot on goal. And here I am, just itching to get a good whack at Peter Puck. When I get through with him, Pete will look like one long skid mark on the highway. That will teach him to stick his nose into places where he isn't wanted."

The third period began. Twenty minutes to play. There was still no score in the game, but the Scouts were getting tired. Their fierce checking and a great performance by goalie Charlie Stopper had kept the Warriors off the scoreboard. But how long would it last? The Warriors had outplayed the Scouts and over two periods had outshot them 30-7.

Suddenly, the Warriors got a break. The Scouts, caught changing their lines while the play was still going on, left a wide path up the center. Three Warriors rushed in. One took Peter Puck on the blade of his stick and slapped him hard at the Scouts' goalie Charlie Stopper. The goalie leaped and stuck out his pad. But Peter bounced off the goal pad and onto the stick of the Warrior wingman who was right there. A quick shot! GOAL!

The Warriors held a 1-0 lead, and the crowd roared for more. As George Phair carried Peter to center ice for the faceoff, Warrior goalie Butch Burns danced around in his goal crease. He was one of the happiest players on the ice.

The blabbermouth goalie yelled at Peter. "Stay away from me, you little rubber rascal. Come around my net and I'll make a flat tire out of you. I'll carve you into a hundred rubber bands. Ho, ho, ho. Hey, Peter! Whatever happened to the Scouts' big scorer, Steve Swift? Are you and Swift not friends any more? You've hardly let him touch you all night."

What Burns had said was close to the truth. Steve Swift had not been able to find skating room. And he hadn't had any good scoring chances.

Swift, skating in to take the faceoff, heard Burns' taunts. There were tight little lines around his eyes and his face started to turn red as the puck was dropped. Swift snapped at Peter with his stick, drew him away from the Warriors' centerman, and dashed off towards the towering Warrior defense pair of Cranston and Simpson. Just as the two bullies moved in on him, Swift let go with a rising slap shot. Simpson screened the shot and goaltender Burns was caught completely by surprise. The puck whistled by his shoulder, smacked off the goal post and bounced into the net. The Scouts had scored! Steve Swift had tied the game for the Scouts at one goal each.

Peter lay in the Warriors' goal, hoping that the referee would rescue him quickly. Peter didn't like the look in Butch Burns' eye. Nor did he like the growling and grumbling that came from behind that scary goalie mask.

"In-grumble-credible. Grumble-growl-lucky-grumble-goal," were the only words that Peter could make out. Then Burns smashed his stick against the goal post and pointed the broken end at Peter. His voice rose to a scream.

"This is your fault," Peter Puck!" he yelled. "Look what you've done! You ruined my shutout, you . . . you . . . you . . ."

Peter stopped him before he could say any more. "Hey, it's not my fault," said Peter, throwing up his arms to protect himself. "I'm just a little hockey puck. Don't blame me. Your job is to stop me. So blame yourself."

With that, Burns swung his broken stick at Peter and sent him flying across

the ice. Peter told George Phair later that it was the first time he had ever had to pull splinters out of his hide.

Back in the goal crease, Butch Burns had a temper tantrum. He sank slowly to his knees and pounded the ice with his gloves.

Meanwhile, the Scouts were back in the game. They had tied the score only seconds after the Warriors had scored the first goal. And just a minute later, Steve Swift struck again. He took a pass, jumped through the defense pair of Simpson and Cranston, skated in on goal and beat Burns with another quick shot. Scouts 2 — Warriors 1. It was so quiet in the arena that Peter thought for a moment he was back in the freezer again.

This time, his pal the referee swooped in and took Peter out of the Warriors' goal mouth before Butch Burns could bash him with his goal stick.

George Phair winked at Peter. "Pretty good shooting, eh, Peter?"

Peter agreed that it was, and winked back.

Butch Burns, in a state of shock, lifted his mask and stared at the score board. His face was as white as his goal mask. He knew that his team was losing the game. His shutout was gone. He'd missed on two shots that he should have stopped. He was getting the jitters in the Warriors' goal.

The Scouts, again led by Steve Swift, scored three more goals near the end of the period. Final score: Scouts 5 — Warriors 1. The Stanley Cup series was tied at three games apiece. After the final buzzer, just as Peter Puck was sliding around the boards at the end of the rink, Butch Burns threw his goal stick at the whirling disc.

"I'll get you yet, Peter Puck," howled the unhappy netminder, waving a huge fist. "And when I catch you I'll squash you so hard you'll look like spilled ink."

2 The Cup is Gone

The next stop was Scout City for the final game of the series. Whoever won this game would win the Stanley Cup.

A couple of hours after the Scouts' big win, Peter Puck was on board a big jet plane. He was resting in the coat pocket of his pal George Phair, the referee, and both were enjoying a smooth flight on their way to Scout City.

Peeking out of the referee's pocket, Peter said, "Thank you, George, for bringing me along with you. You don't know how hard it is for me to make all of my own travel arrangements."

"That's all right," the referee replied. "You may not realize it, old friend, but referees always like working with a hockey puck that plays the game fair and square. Believe me, Peter, you're number one with us. You never gripe about going into the freezer, you're always on time, and you don't complain when guys like Butch Burns whack you around. You hardly ever give us officials a problem by hopping in and out of a goal net so we might miss a

score. Some pucks give us all sorts of trouble, Pete. You know . . . taking bad bounces, flying into the crowd all the time . . . things like that. Not you, Pete. You take the game seriously. You're a real pro. So the least I can do is to make sure you get to Scout City in time for the big game tomorrow. I'll take you right to the arena when we get there, and tuck you in the freezer for the night. Then you'll be well rested for the final game of the year."

"You're a swell guy, George," said Peter. "I just wish all the players knew you like I know you. Then they'd never say some of the things they say about you when you're working a game."

"Aw, they don't mean most of those things," laughed the referee.

"But what about a guy like Butch Burns? After the game tonight he threatened me. Do you think he meant it?"

George Phair frowned, thinking over the question. Then he said, "I wouldn't worry too much about Butch. He's a mean fellow with a nasty temper, but right now I think he's got more important things on his mind . . . like how the Warriors will cope with Steve Swift tomorrow night. And now, Peter, slide back down into my pocket and try to get a little sleep. Big game tomorrow."

Peter did as the referee suggested, sliding down into the pocket and

yawning. But he couldn't sleep. He was too excited about tomorrow's game
. . . the seventh and deciding game between the Scouts and the Warriors.

As promised, George Phair took Peter Puck from the airport in Scout City
to Big League Arena, the huge home of the Scouts.

The arena was all locked up when they arrived, but there was a special door
with a buzzer on it. George Phair rang the buzzer. A few seconds later a
security guard let them in.

The guard's name was Jess Jackson. He led them down dark halls toward the room with the freezer in it. As they passed through the arena lobby, Peter noticed a large glass case with a gleaming trophy on a pedestal inside. He stopped, attracted by the shining metal. Both the security guard and George Phair stopped too.

"Is that what I think it is?" asked Peter. "Is that *really* the Stanley Cup in there?"

His friends laughed.

"That's it," said Jess the guard.

"That's the Stanley Cup, all right," said the referee. "It's a beauty, isn't it? All shined up and ready to be presented to the winner tomorrow. You know, Peter, hockey men have been scrambling to win that trophy since 1894. Some people have spent millions of dollars trying to get hold of that old mug. And what a history it has. It's been damaged, stolen, lost and tarnished. One night long ago, it was left on a street corner in Montreal after a playoff game. Some players stopped to change a flat tire on their car and left the cup on the curb

when they finished. Another time, some people say, an Ottawa player kicked it into the Rideau Canal as a prank. Luckily, the canal was frozen, and the cup was dug out of the snow the next day."

"Will it be all right here . . . tonight?" asked Peter Puck.

"It sure will," said the guard. "Old Jess here is taking good care of Lord Stanley's famous cup. That showcase is locked tight and I have the key right here." Jess patted his pants pocket.

The three of them continued their trek through the shadowy halls, until they reached the room where the freezer was kept.

George Phair lifted Peter into the freezer and said, "I don't envy you, Pete, spending the night in there. I wouldn't last ten minutes."

Peter Puck grinned. "The freezer's not so bad, George. It's cold, all right, but I'm used to it. Besides, after being chased around a hockey rink for a couple of hours, it's one place a guy can find a little peace and quiet. Well, thanks for everything. Good night, Jess. Good night, George."

The two men left Peter in his modern-day igloo and walked back to the arena entrance. Then Jess locked up and returned to the lobby to guard the Stanley Cup.

In the freezer, meanwhile, Peter closed his eyes and relaxed. It had been an exciting day. He thought again of riding Steve Swift's blistering slapshot, right into the goal behind Butch Burns. He frowned when he recalled the goalie's threats. He rubbed his round rubber body where Burns had belted him with his broken goal stick. Hockey players are rugged, he thought, but so are hockey pucks. He took pride in the thought. Hockey was his only love, and he wouldn't change his life for any other. Even when it came to spending all those hours in the freezer where, as referee George Phair once said, it was as chilly as a polar bear's kiss.

Chilly? That's funny, thought Peter. It doesn't seem to be chilly in here tonight. As a matter of fact, suddenly it's not chilly at all. He looked around, knowing something was wrong. Water was dripping down the freezer wall. There was something *very* wrong. Then it dawned on Peter. The freezer wasn't working properly. It was getting warm . . . very warm. It was getting . . . hot! Peter jumped up in alarm. He pounded on the freezer door with his tiny fists. Nobody would hear that, he thought.

Looking around, he spied a hockey stick leaning against the freezer wall. Grabbing it, he smashed the stick against the door. Bang! Bang! Bang! "Help, somebody!" shouted Peter. "Get me out of here! I can't breathe!"

Suddenly, the freezer door burst open and there was the guard. Jess grabbed Peter Puck and lifted him out. He placed Peter on the floor a safe distance away and then raced back to the freezer.

Peter could now see why he had felt so hot. A fire was blazing in front of
the freezer. Broken hockey sticks were burning, sending flame and smoke up

the freezer wall. Jess yanked a fire extinguisher off the wall, turned it on the blaze, and in seconds the flames were out.

"Pardon me for saying so, Jess," said Peter, catching his breath, "but the freezer room is hardly the place to be burning old hockey sticks. I wish you'd speak to the careless fellow who started that blaze. And by the way, thanks for coming to my rescue when you did. If it hadn't been for you, my little rubber body would look like liquid shoe polish right now."

Jess looked solemnly at Peter. "My friend," he said, "there's nobody but you and me in the arena tonight. At least, there's not supposed to be. And nobody's allowed to burn hockey sticks or anything else in here. What I'm saying, Peter Puck, is that somebody started that fire . . . on purpose."

"You mean . . ."

"What I mean, Peter, is that somebody was trying to make sure that you'd end up like something a fellow could pour down a drain."

Peter's rubber skin prickled. Somebody was trying to hurt him . . . on purpose. It was a scary thought.

Crash! Thump! Whump!

"What was that?" cried Peter, catching Jess by the arm.

"That was the showcase," shouted Jess, darting for the door. "Somebody's broken the glass. Somebody's trying to grab the Stanley Cup. Come on. Maybe we can catch him."

Peter Puck and Jess raced down the dark hall. Ahead of them, they heard footsteps echo through the arena. Someone was running away.

They burst into the lobby and found themselves sidestepping big pieces of broken glass. Sure enough, the glass case housing the Stanley Cup was shattered. And the cup was gone.

"This way!" shouted Jess, turning down a gloomy ramp that led to the outside. "He can't get far carrying that big thing. We'll get him yet."

Jess sped off. Peter, short legs churning, was only a few strides behind.

The ramp was in almost total darkness, but the pair raced on, hot on the trail of the man who was running away with the Stanley Cup.

Ahead of him, Peter Puck saw Jess spin around a corner. There was a cry of surprise and a flash of metal. Peter heard a heavy clunk and Jess staggered back.

"Are you all right, Jess?" asked Peter when he caught up. "What happened?"

The guard rubbed his head. "He slugged me," muttered Jess. "Hit me with the cup. My head is still ringing. Gotta sit down for a second. Now we'll never catch that guy."

"I'll go after him, Jess. You take it easy."

"Be careful, Peter," Jess warned. "I got a glimpse of him. He's big and mean and he's wearing a mask."

But Peter was racing off. He flew down the ramp, and heard a lot of noise somewhere ahead of him. In the dim light he spotted a huge shadowy figure trying to open a side door. There were grunts as the man heaved against the door, trying to break the lock. Just as Peter arrived on the scene, the man

grabbed a mop from a nearby pail and swung it wildly over his head.

Peter tried to skid to a halt but he couldn't stop. The mop came down with a whack! Peter took the full force of the mop and was sent skidding and tumbling across the hallway. Then, before he could get up again, the man lifted the empty pail and plopped it over Peter's head. But just as the pail came down over him, Peter caught sight of the man's outline in the shadows. The face was hidden behind a mask, a white mask that completely hid the man's features. For just a second Peter saw a flash of red and then . . . darkness.

"Let me out of here!" hollered Peter. "Stop thief!"

Peter banged the inside of the pail until his tiny knuckles were bruised and swollen.

Moments later, the bucket was lifted, and there stood Jess.

"What happened, Pete? Did the crook get away?"

"It looks that way, Jess. He whacked me with a mop handle and slammed the pail over my head. He moves fast, Jess. And look here! He forced the lock on the door with the mop handle and made his getaway. We've lost him now for sure, Jess."

"And he's got the Stanley Cup," Jess said sadly. "I'll sure catch it from the league officials now. And just wait till the newspapers hear about this."

3 Peter is a Hero

It wasn't long before *everybody* knew about the theft of the Stanley Cup. Jess and Peter phoned the police and in a matter of minutes a squad of detectives arrived. Reporters and photographers followed, a film cameraman and a TV newsman dashed around, setting up lights and asking for statements. A chubby little man, still wearing pyjamas and slippers but with a topcoat thrown over his shoulders, arrived blinking and breathless and introduced himself as Mr. Gordon from NHL security.

"Oh, my!" he said gravely, examining a piece of broken glass and peering inside the empty showcase as if, somehow, the cup might still be there. "Oh, my," he repeated, "this will never do. No, this will never do at all."

Then he took Peter Puck and Jess Jackson aside and asked a lot of questions about the robbery. Peter was quick to explain how Jess was busy saving his life when the thief stole the cup.

"Don't blame Jess for leaving his post, Mr. Gordon," urged Peter. "He's a real hero. If Jess hadn't come along when he did I'd be a dead duck . . . I mean puck."

The newspapers, as Jess had predicted, told the whole story about the robbery. There was even a photo of Jess and Peter on the front page of the *News*. There was another photo of the empty showcase with broken glass all around it. The *Daily Journal* had the best story:

Scout City: The Stanley Cup, pro hockey's biggest prize, was stolen late last night. The valuable trophy was taken from a locked glass show-case at the Scout City Arena in a daring robbery that left a guard in-jured and hockey star Peter Puck shaken up.

Scout City police admit that they have few clues in the case. Jess Jackson, the guard, and Peter Puck could only give a vague description of the thief. They say he wore a white mask and dark clothing.

The theft took place while Jackson was fighting a small fire in the building, a blaze that threatened the life of hockey star Peter Puck, who was trapped in a nearby freezer. Peter Puck called Mr. Jackson's quick action in putting out the blaze "a real lifesaver." The famous hockey puck and the guard chased the thief through the arena and both were shaken up in separate scuffles with the robber.

Mr. Jackson called Peter Puck "the bravest little guy around. He chased that big fellow right out of the building."

The incident is not expected to keep Peter Puck out of the lineup when the Scouts meet the Warriors tonight in the deciding game of the Stanley Cup playoffs.

The cup was to be presented to the winners tonight. League President James Boyd has asked for the safe return of the famous trophy. He said that he was "deeply concerned" over the matter and expressed fears that he might soon receive a demand for a huge ransom.

The investigation continues.

Back in the freezer once again, Peter Puck thought over the events of the past 24 hours. Why would anyone steal the Stanley Cup, he wondered. It would certainly not be easy to sell. Mr. Boyd was probably right, he decided. The thief would no doubt contact the league and demand a large ransom for the safe return of the trophy.

Sometimes I wish I was bigger and stronger, thought Peter. Then I could have stopped the thief. And I wish I'd been able to tell the police what the man looked like. I remember a white mask and a flash of red. Let me think . . . is there anything else? No. I guess that's all I can recall and there's not much more that I can do about it now. It's almost time for the big game. Even without the cup, the series must go on.

And with that, Peter began thinking about the final game of the season. He turned his thoughts inward and began to concentrate on his own performance. This was something that Peter did before every hockey match. I must stay flat on the ice and give the players a chance to whack me around, he told himself. And even though I'd like to fly over the boards and keep myself safe, I must try to remain in play. Of course, there are times when I simply can't help what happens to me, especially when fellows like Steve Swift get hold of me. And, oh, yes, I must fall fairly between the sticks on the faceoffs. The players get angry with me when they think that I let the other guy steal me away first. It's not as easy as people think, sighed Peter, being the world's number one hockey puck.

There was a knock at the freezer door.

"Hey, Peter! Up and at 'em! It's game time!"

It was the voice of Peter's friend George Phair.

"Hi, George. I didn't expect to see you here," said Peter as the freezer door was swung open.

"Neither did I," said the referee, picking Peter up and brushing small icicles off his hard little body. "I was supposed to be the spare official tonight, but I

was told at the last minute that I was to be referee for the game. Referee Bill Jones stepped out of a taxi and twisted his ankle, so I'm elected. Surprise, huh?"

It was a surprise. It was unusual for the same referee to be in charge of two playoff games in a row. But Peter was pleased to see his old friend wearing the striped referee's shirt and uniform.

4 The Final Game

The huge arena was buzzing with excitement when Peter and the referee skated to center ice. Peter drew a huge round of applause from the fans. They had read about his early morning adventures and appreciated his game attempt to save the Stanley Cup.

Then the Warriors and Scouts lined up along their own blue lines. The National Anthem was played, and seconds later the game began.

Peter could tell right away that it was going to be an exciting game. And probably a close one. Both teams wanted to jump into an early lead. Skates flashed across the ice as the players chased after Peter. Chips of ice and snow flew up as they cut quickly, forechecking and backchecking. Peter could hear the grunts as bodies smacked together in the corners. He could hear the sighs of disappointment when shots on goal failed to go in, the heavy breathing as lines were changed and players moved to the bench, where they slumped over, heads down, resting. Soon they were ready to get back out on the ice again and try for a score.

The goaltending was superb — at both ends. The crowd clapped loudly time after time for Charlie Stopper as he turned aside the Warrior scoring drives. Late in the period, when the Scouts had a penalty and were short-handed, Stopper took a blistering shot on the chest from Crash Cranston, the Warrior defenseman. The rebound came bouncing out, right onto the stick of Slugger Simpson, the other Warrior defenseman. He fired, and Stopper leaped for the puck. Too late. It hit the upper corner. The red light went on. Goal! The Warriors led 1-0.

The Warriors pounded Simpson on the back while the Scout fans groaned.

Butch Burns danced in the Warrior goal crease and raised his goal stick high in the air. A victory salute.

This move caught the eye of Steve Swift, the Scouts' forward, who muttered, "It's a little early for that," as the players lined up for the faceoff.

As hard as he tried, Swift could not get through the Warriors' defense for the rest of his shift on the ice. Nor could his team mates. Simpson and Cranston, the Warriors' tough defensemen, played rougher than they had all season. Trying to protect their one-goal lead, they took the puck away from every Scout who came near.

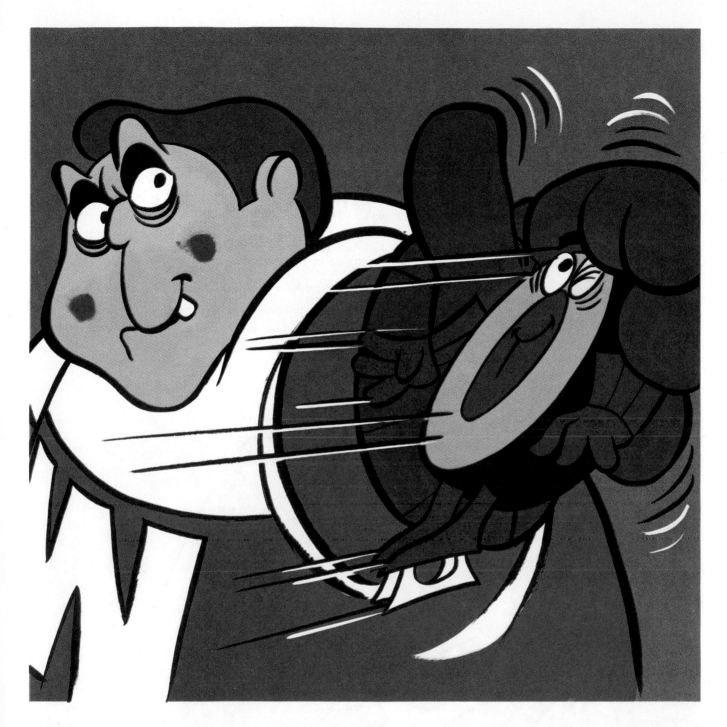

Things were much the same in the second period, and the Scout fans were beginning to despair. Swift managed two hard shots on goal. On one shot Peter thought for a second that he might slip by Butch Burns, but the steady Burns plucked him out of the air just before he crossed the goal line.

"Got you, you rascal!" shouted Burns. "And here's what I do to hockey pucks that try to sneak into my net." He wound up and threw Peter against the boards at the end of the rink. Then, as Peter bounced away, Burns reached out with his stick and flipped Peter high in the air . . . up . . . up . . . up, as high as the big clock over center ice. Then, spinning and twisting, Peter started

back down, picking up speed. And there, waiting for him with his large goal stick raised high in the air, was Butch Burns.

Peter tried to twist away at the last second, but there was no way that he could get away from Butch Burns. The huge stick lashed out and wha-a-a-ck! A direct hit! Burns had swung his goal stick like a baseball bat and sent Peter screaming toward the boards. There was no time for Peter to brace himself.

Crun-u-nch! Peter hit the boards with a loud crash and sank slowly to the ice. He gasped for breath and tears came to his eyes. Most of the time, the knocks and whacks that Peter took on the hockey rink didn't bother him. He had a tough hide and enjoyed being the center of the action. But Burns had tried to injure him on purpose. Even the referee, George Phair, saw it that way.

Phair helped Peter Puck pick himself up. "You okay, kid?" he asked. The referee looked very concerned.

"I . . . I guess so," groaned Peter. "Just had the wind knocked out of me."

"Burns deserves a penalty for that," said George. "He could have hurt you with that blow."

"But, George, you can't give him a penalty," said Peter. "There's nothing in the rule book that says you can't belt a hockey puck around. That's what the game is all about, isn't it? You'd look pretty silly giving him a penalty for that, George."

"Yeah, I guess you're right. Still, I hate to see that bully get away with it."

"Don't worry, ref, I can look after myself. Now, face me off over here in the corner and we'll get on with the game."

The referee did as Peter told him. They both glared at the Warriors' burly goalie, who roared with laughter from behind his mask.

The game moved into the third period with the Warriors holding on to their 1-0 lead. Every second moved them closer to the championship.

With two minutes to play, the Scouts seemed to be finished. There was a faceoff at center ice and Steve Swift turned to Peter while they waited for the Warrior centerman to get a new stick at the bench.

"I'm afraid we've had it," sighed Swift. "I'm so tired that I can barely stand up. And that Burns . . . he's stopped my high, hard ones all night. And now we're running out of time."

"Don't give up, Steve. A real pro never gives up. And you've always been a real pro, in my opinion. You must have enough strength left for one more good shot. And don't worry about hurting me. It would be a pleasure to beat a guy like Butch Burns if you did the scoring."

Swift gave Peter a quick little grin. "Thanks, pal," he said, as George Phair moved in to drop the puck.

Swift threw his shoulder into the Warriors' center and bowled him over. He grabbed the loose puck with his stick and whirled in on the defense pair of Simpson and Cranston. They waited for him . . . waited to pound him to the ice. Just as he hit the blue line, Swift stopped suddenly. For just a second, it looked like he didn't want any part of the rough Simpson and the rougher Cranston.

"We've got him!" screamed Simpson.

"He's scared stiff!" Cranston shouted. They lunged at Swift, anxious to hit the unmoving target.

As they started after him, Swift moved. He dipped his shoulder and darted into the small opening between the giant defensemen. What a move! He had fooled them completely by pretending to be afraid. Now, in full flight, he raced in on the crouching Burns. He thought about Peter Puck's words . . . you must have one good shot left . . . don't worry about hurting me.

Swift's stick blade flashed back . . . high over his shoulder. It came sailing down . . . connected squarely with Peter Puck . . . and flashed him at an unbelievable speed toward the waiting Warrior goalie.

Burns never had a chance. Peter sailed past his mask, missing an ear by less than an inch, and smacked into the net. It was a goal! The game was tied. The

Scout fans went wild. Programs sailed down to the ice. Peter lay back in the net, happy that Steve Swift had found the strength for one more good shot.

He didn't sit there for long. Butch Burns, furious that a goal had been scored on him, squeezed Peter in his huge hand. He pulled him out of the net and reared back, flinging the weary puck at the glass backboards at the end of the rink. Cla-a-ng!

Peter hit the glass and bounced back, flipping high into the air. He came to rest right on top of the goal. Because of the net, it was a soft landing, and Peter lay there, catching his breath.

5 Peter Unmasks the Thief

Butch Burns, meanwhile, had turned back to his goal. He didn't see Peter directly behind him, right behind his head.

Peter looked up. He was within inches of Butch Burns' neck. He could see Burns' long hair pushing out of the back of his face mask. He could see the edges of the mask and under the hair . . . the red straps holding the mask in place. He could see . . .

"Red straps," said Peter in a tiny voice. Where had he seen red straps like the ones on Burns' mask? Then it came to him. The man who'd stolen the

Stanley Cup had a mask on . . . and it was held on with red straps. That was the flash of red Peter had seen just as the bucket came down over his head in the dark arena when he was chasing the thief.

"My gosh," Peter said, scrambling off the top of the net and jumping into the arms of referee Phair.

"Burns did it, George! Do something! Arrest him! Handcuff him! Don't let him get away!"

"What in the world are you talking about, Peter? What are you so excited about?"

"Butch Burns is the thief, George. The guy who stole the Stanley Cup. I saw a guy wearing a white mask with red straps. I just saw the straps holding Burns' mask in place and they're red. I know he's the thief. Stop him before he gets away!"

"Now wait a second, Pete. Even if you're right, and Burns is the thief, I can't do anything now. Listen to that crowd. They want us to get on with the game. There's only thirty seconds to play. We'll have to talk about this later. Now let's play hockey."

Thirty seconds. Peter was so excited that he could hardly hold still for the

faceoff. But he managed somehow. And there was Steve Swift's stick grabbing him on the first bounce, bringing him across the center ice red line, passing Peter to a wing. Then Swift skated faster, took Peter on a return pass, pushed him ahead a few feet and with a burst of speed sailed past two Warriors who were trying to take the puck away.

Simpson tried to cut Swift off at the blue line, but Swift was in full flight and in no mood to be stopped. He deked around Simpson, leaped over Crash Cranston who had flung himself in Swift's path. Somehow Peter slid under Cranston's falling body. Then Swift took Peter on his stick again, moved him ahead a few feet, and wound up for a slapshot. The stick flashed back, came down in an arc, and Butch Burns made his desperate move. He flung himself out of the goal, dove in front of Steve Swift, and tried to smother the shot before Swift took it. But this was just what Swift was waiting for. He had faked the slapshot and had lured Burns out of the goal. Now the Warrior goalie saw the trap. He tried to scramble back, but too late. Swift calmly drew away from the helpless Burns, stepped around him, and lifted Peter Puck into the Warriors' empty goal.

The Scout fans roared as the red light flashed, signaling a goal. Then the green light flashed, telling everyone that the game was over. A last-second goal by Steve Swift of the Scouts had won the game and the Stanley Cup.

Scout players spilled off the bench. They swarmed around the grinning Swift and slapped him on the back. They messed his hair, and Charlie Stopper, the Scout goalie, even kissed him on the cheek.

Peter Puck, who had bounced out of the Warriors' goal after the winning score, was caught up in the excitement as well. He watched the crowd go wild, saw the players jump over the boards. He saw George Phair skate over to scoop him up and keep him from being trampled.

As the referee came near, Peter heard him shout.

"Look out, Peter! Look out behind you!"

Peter turned just in time to see Butch Burns coming after him, waving his big fists in the air. He was going to take one last crack at Peter Puck.

"I'll fix you, Peter Puck," roared the rushing goalie. "I missed you last night, but I'll get you this time."

Tired as he was, Peter zipped down the ice, his tiny body just inches ahead of the goalie. Players scattered, startled by the sight. At center ice, Peter looked back. Burns was catching up fast.

At the blue line, Peter made up his mind quickly. He stopped, catching Burns by surprise. Burns tried to stop too, but his heavy goalie equipment kept him moving. Then Peter darted in front of one of Burns' skates.

Crash! Burns spilled to the ice, losing one glove. His huge body skidded forward, out of control. Head first, he skidded along, ten, twenty, thirty feet, right into the empty net at the end of the rink.

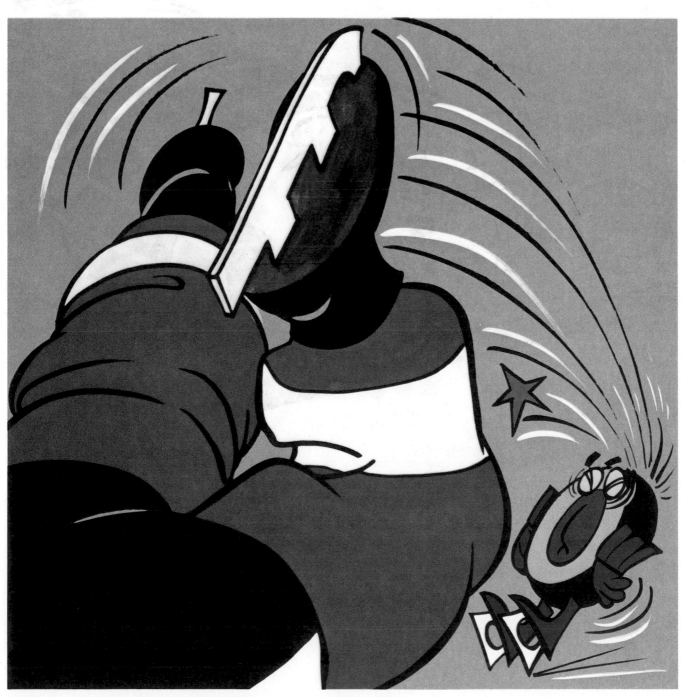

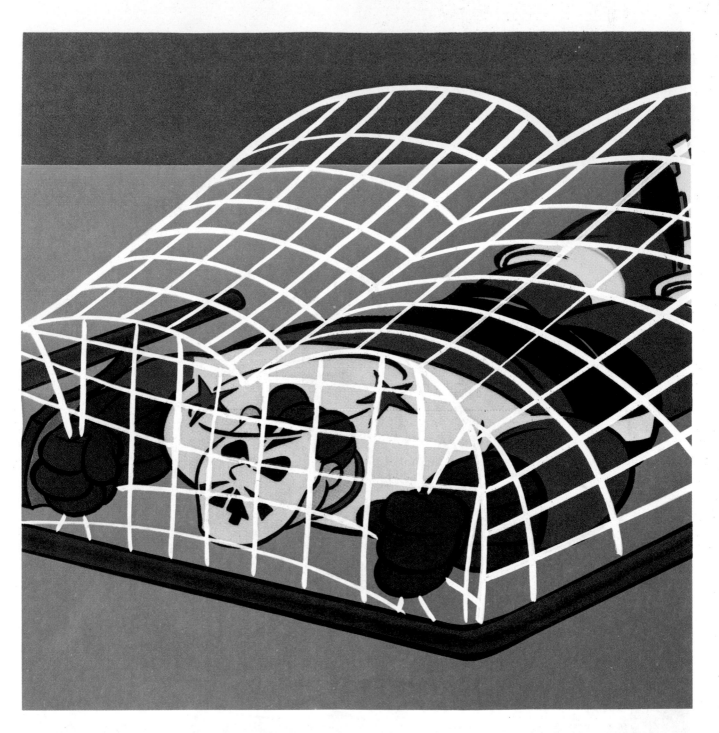

Br-u-ump! Burns hit the back of the net so hard that the goal came loose from the ice. As thousands of people watched, the net bounced in the air, then slowly toppled over, trapping the dazed goalie. He lay there, netted, like a lobster in a trap.

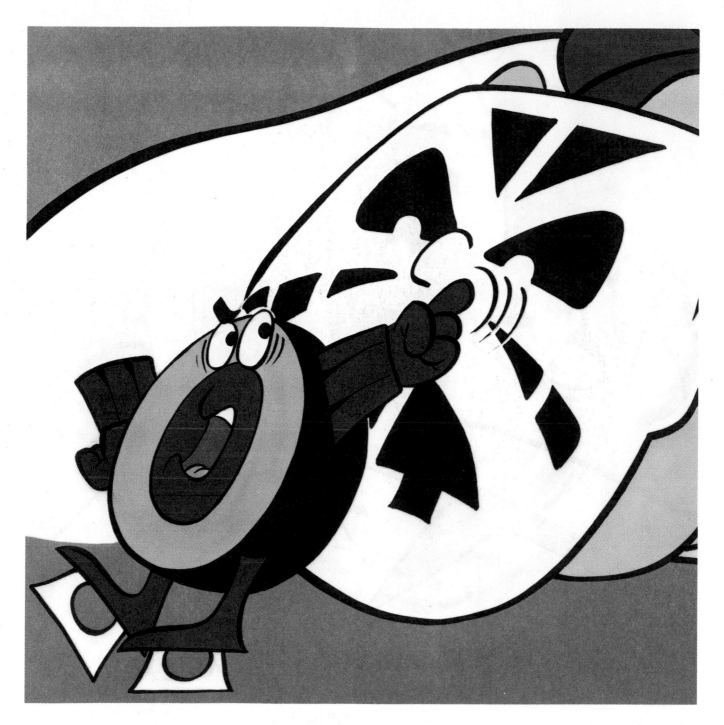

Peter Puck leaped into action. He sped across the ice and flipped himself up on the overturned net.

Peter peered down through the netting at Butch Burns. The referee, the linesmen, players and officials crowded around.

"Gotcha now, Mr. Burns," cried Peter, as if his few ounces were the only thing between the trapped goalie and freedom. "I know you stole the Stanley Cup. I recognized your face mask with the red straps. And you're not getting out of here until you admit it."

The goaltender pulled off his face mask and looked up at Peter. He looked around at all the people watching him, sighed once, and said, "Okay, Pete. You win. I admit I stole the cup. And I'll tell you why. The way Steve Swift and his team played in the last game I thought the Warriors didn't have a chance to win it fair and square. I've never won the Stanley Cup, Pete, and you know how much that means to a hockey player. I just wanted to keep the cup for a while and return it somehow. Then you and that guard had to mix in . . ."

"Oh, yeah? Then why did you try to trap me in that freezer, Butch? You were trying to roast me, weren't you? Why, I almost became a . . . a puckburger."

"No, Pete, that was all a mistake. Really it was. You see, I started the fire so that the guard would come running. While he was busy putting out the fire I figured I'd slip off with the Stanley Cup. I forgot all about you being in the freezer. Honest I did, Pete. I know I've got a nasty temper but I never planned to hurt you. I'm sorry about the fire and I'm sorry about taking the cup and I'm sorry I knocked you around in the game tonight."

"Well, you should be, Butch," said Peter Puck. "I just hope that the police believe your story. You've got to play fair, you know, both off and on the ice. By the way, Butch, where *is* the Stanley Cup?"

"It's right outside in the parking lot, Pete. I hid it in the trunk of a car I borrowed. And not a mark on it, Pete. Honest!"

85

The Scout players heard this, and sent their trainer and manager out to get the trophy which they had played so hard to win. They were back in minutes, and a great roar from the crowd went up when the cup was spotted.

Then Mr. Boyd, the NHL President, was handed a microphone and in a brief ceremony, presented the cup to Steve Swift, the smiling captain of the Scouts. Swift made a brief speech and, holding the cup over his head, skated slowly around the arena. Cheers rained down, and flashbulbs popped everywhere.

As Steve Swift skated past a smiling Peter Puck, he winked and said, "Peter, we're the champs this year, but you're a champ every year, in every game. Now hop up here and I'll take you for a ride. We might not have this trophy if it wasn't for you."

Then Peter Puck, so proud that he thought he would burst out of his rubber skin, took a great leap and landed right in the bowl of the Stanley Cup. The cheers filled the arena, and Peter waved until his little arms ached as Steve Swift paraded him around the ice surface.

Hockey, thought Peter Puck, is the greatest game of all.

I hope you enjoyed this book. Watch for my other fascinating book, *Peter Puck's Greatest Moments in Hockey.*

And coming soon, another exciting adventure story in the life of the world's most famous hockey puck—that's me, guys and girls, the imp of the ice.

Peter Puck